White
Man
Dreaming

a novella by

F. M. Cipriano

FMC Press

White Man Dreaming

[ISBN 978-0-9941743-6-9]
First published 2018 by FMC Press
PO Box 13179
Law Courts VIC 8010
Australia
Copyright © F. M. Cipriano 2018
Book Cover Design: Jelena Gajic
Editing and Proofreading: Kerry Davies

A catalogue record for this book is available from the National Library of Australia

This book, other than Part 2: The Notes, is a fact-based fiction. Names and characters, other than public figures, are the product of the author's imagination or are used fictitiously. Any resemblance to actual persons, living or dead, is coincidental. No responsibility can be accepted by the publisher or author for any damages resulting from the misrepresentation of this work by associating any resemblances to any factual person, living or dead. All care has been taken in the preparation of the information herein, but no responsibility can be accepted by the publisher or author for any damages resulting from the misinterpretation of this work. All contact details given in this book were current at the time of publication, but are subject to change.

Published by FMC Press

www.fmcpress.com

Front Cover Flag

The front cover features a flag that brings together elements of the Aboriginal flag, the Torres Strait Islander flag and the Australian flag.

The Aboriginal flag is represented by red earth and black Aboriginal people of Australia. The Torres Strait Islander flag is represented by green land, blue waters and black Torres Strait Islanders. The Australian flag is represented by five stars typifying the constellation of the Southern Cross.

The Australian flag also features the Seven Point Star, referred to as the Commonwealth Star, also known as the Federation Star. The seven points represent the six original states of the Commonwealth of Australia with the seventh point representing the territories and any future states of Australia.

The flag on the front cover adopts the five white stars typifying the constellation of the Southern Cross as well as a white eight point star, which represents a point for each of the six states and the two territories of Australia. It is referred to as the Republican Star. More importantly, the white stars in the black sky symbolise reconciliation between black and white Australians.

Table of Contents

About the Author

F. M. Cipriano (Frank) was born in Melbourne, Australia. He has a Bachelor of Business, a Graduate Diploma in Accounting and a Master of Taxation.

Frank was a career public servant with the Australian Taxation Office (ATO) until he gained a voluntary redundancy, departing on 29 August 2014.

Since leaving the ATO, Frank has pursued his passion for writing. His other published books are: *A Bachelor's Travels*, *My Taxing Career* and *A Working Holiday*.

White Man Dreaming is a novella inspired by a trip Frank took to outback Australia in 1986, which had a profound impact that transformed his attitude towards the country of his birth.

Other Books by the Author

A Bachelor's Travels

Roland is a single, 27-year-old public servant who lives with his parents. He enjoyed life until most of his mates got married, which results in a solo overseas trip that triggers a lifelong obsession. He wanders the globe, through the continents of Europe, Africa, Asia and the Americas. His journeys range from painstaking itinerant travel to the serendipity of spontaneous adventures, involving a plethora of unique experiences that enrich his knowledge, augment his appreciation of different cultures, impact his attitudes and uplift his spirits. However, approaching middle age, Roland feels it may be time for his overseas travels to come to an end. Is it time to open a new chapter in his life and settle down to a comfortable existence in Australia? It is a question he wrestles with until circumstances ultimately decide his course.

Other Books by the Author

My Taxing Career

Fred Campari had no intention of being employed by the Tax Office but, ironically, that's where he ended up. He developed a liking for his work and concerted his efforts to make a positive difference; however, he was constantly stymied and frustrated by the actions of senior management. The Tax Office seemed to have developed a culture that encouraged and rewarded backstabbers, informers and lackeys. In fact, these qualities appeared to be prerequisites to staff advancement. Fred eventually resigned himself to the fact that he had reached the peak of his career but he had not bargained for a possible fall when an attack by senior executives would threaten his very survival.

*   *   *

"When I was a kid, I was asked what I wanted to do when I grew up. I replied that I wanted to join the circus. Oddly enough, by joining the Tax Office, I sort of did."

Fred Campari

Other Books by the Author

A Working Holiday

John and Con are two computer science graduates whose friendship began at their alma mater; a friendship that further developed when they gained graduate positions with the same information technology company.

However, their friendship is put to the test after they embark on an overseas trip of a lifetime.

Returning to work in Australia, the two come face-to-face. It is an encounter with surprising consequences.

Will they be able to re-ignite their friendship?

Or will their friendship be broken forever?

Only time will tell.

PART 1

THE STORY BEGINS

Chapter 1

The Start of Gap Years

Bitter cold and rain greeted the early-morning workers, who numbered in their dozens, as they assembled behind the freight company's barbed-wire fence.

Competition was fierce as only one in five of them would be picked to work. It was a daily routine that tested the most hardened souls.

Art Costello was squeezed into the middle of the crowd of workers. He was of average height and weight but appeared diminutive surrounded by the burly men.

The gates opened and Art was buffeted and

crushed from all directions as the workers jockeyed for a prominent position. He wasn't expecting to be selected but, as several of the men around him were picked, so was he.

The selected workers were making their way to the storage sheds when a man pulled Art aside.

"Where the fuck do you think you're going?" the man demanded to know.

"I was selected to work," Art responded.

"Well I'm the foreman and we don't need you today so you can get lost."

Art meekly made his way back to his rented one-bedroom flat in Footscray – a working-class suburb in western Melbourne.

Trying to figure out what he was going to do for the rest of the day, Art reflected on whether it was such a good idea to have self-imposed gap years between the end of his law degree and the commencement of a graduate position.

I'm really hitting the bottom of the barrel getting up at four o'clock in the morning just to find out whether I have work for the day, Art thought. But he was sure, though, that the physical work would give him mental toughness and a sense of achievement.

Art returned to the company the following day. He assembled behind the barbed-wire fence, positioning himself in the same location he stood the day before. Again, he wasn't hopeful of being selected, but he was.

Art followed the workers as they made their way to the storage sheds and noticed the foreman walking towards him. He was expecting to be pulled aside again but the foreman stopped and just looked on.

Once in the storage shed, the workers were assigned various jobs. There were only two men remaining and one of them was Art. The other man had a strong, stocky build and appeared to be of middle age. They were both assigned the job of unloading bags of malt grain.

"My name's Hamish," the man said with a gruff, Scottish accent.

"Hi, I'm Art."

"Is this your first time labouring?" Hamish asked.

"I'm afraid it is," Art advised.

"That's okay," Hamish reassured him. "I'll watch your back."

The two men got to work, with Hamish showing Art how to unload the 25-kilogram bags of malt from a railway wagon and onto pallets, which were forklifted onto trucks.

Art looked on as Hamish bounced into the railway wagon, grabbed hold of a top corner of two bags – one bag per hand – and dragged them to the doorway of the wagon, where he stood them upright.

Hamish leapt out of the railway wagon and grabbed one of the bags by its side and tugged at it. The weight of the bag caused it to topple over and he controlled it so that it nestled smoothly onto his shoulder. He then marched over, about a dozen paces, where he neatly placed the bag on a pallet.

Art was still looking on, wide-eyed and with growing admiration, as Hamish returned to the railway wagon where he repeated the process with the second bag.

"So that's how it's done," Hamish asserted. "Got it?"

"Yep," Art replied, nodding affirmatively.

Art sprang into the railway wagon, where he grabbed hold of a top corner of two bags – – one bag per hand – just as Hamish had done. He attempted to drag them, but the moment he felt the weight of the bags, they caused a jolt on his arms. His effort was strained and his progress was slow, so he left one of the bags and dragged the other by both hands to the doorway of the railway wagon and stood the bag upright.

Art jumped out of the railway wagon and almost fell over as his feet hit the concrete floor. He had to steady himself before he aligned his body in front of the bag. He gave Hamish a passing glance and a wry smile as he grabbed hold of the bag and tugged at it.

The bag toppled over and, although Art tried to control it, the bag's weight caused it to accelerate downward, clipping the side of his head, grazing his ear and crashing down onto his shoulder.

Again, Art had to steady himself before he staggered over to the pallet, where he dumped the bag. It hit the pallet with a thud and he ended up falling on top of it. He then got up and brushed himself off.

Art hesitantly looked over to Hamish, who was looking back with an expression of utter amazement and disbelief.

"You need to ensure that the bags don't extend beyond the edge of the pallet," Hamish advised. "You also need to stack the bags tightly in an interlocking pattern to reduce the risk of them shifting during transit."

"By the way," Hamish added as he was making his way back to the railway wagon, "be very careful of the iron hooks hanging around. You wouldn't want to cut yourself on one of those."

They got to work and Art struggled to keep up with Hamish in an effort to complete his share of the load.

Art tried to pick up his pace, but found that it caused him to become unbalanced and stumble all over the place. The bags' repeated pounding onto his shoulder made him feel as if he was knocking himself senseless and the continual rasping of the hessian bags with their coarse and scratchy texture against his ear caused severe chaffing.

After a while, Art's ear became numb. He attempted to ameliorate his ordeal by alternating shoulders but all this seemed to achieve was a pounding to both sides of his head and having both his ears chaffed and numb.

There was a loud whistle and Art was relieved to learn that it was the call for lunch.

Art staggered over to the sandwich bar while Hamish munched on his own food.

"We've still got quite a bit to go," Art commented to Hamish when he returned from the shop.

"We'll be right," Hamish said confidently.

They recommenced work with Hamish picking up the pace. Art tried to keep up, but he could only manage to unload one bag for every two that Hamish unloaded. Hamish then unexpectedly stepped away.

"Hey, Murray!" Hamish shouted.

A man appeared and Art turned to see the foreman who had sent him away the day before.

"You might want to check on Art,"

Hamish suggested.

Murray's eyes followed a trail of blood that emanated from Art's bloodied ear. He took a closer look to witness Art's ear lobe ripped open.

"I'll take you to the first aid room," Murray stated. "We can't have you bleeding all over the place."

After medical treatment, Art returned to the storage shed.

"How's it going?" Hamish asked.

"I'm fine," Art replied. "Even after your warning, I still managed to rip my ear lobe on one of the iron hooks."

Art jumped into the railway wagon to find it empty.

"Did you manage to unload the rest of the bags on your own?"

Hamish's response was nonchalant. "Aye."

Chapter 2

Hard Labour

Getting into the swing of the job, Art gained a reputation for being a hard worker and was regularly selected to pair off with Hamish to undertake the labour-intensive work. They developed into a productive unit, as well as developing a good friendship.

"If you've got a law degree why didn't you get a job with a legal firm?" Hamish asked.

"I was a little disillusioned and wasn't sure what I wanted to do," Art responded. "I felt I needed to take some time off to experience other aspects of life."

"A good and secure job is one of the most

important things in life," Hamish opined.

"How did you end up doing labouring work?" asked Art.

Hamish was pensive and seemingly unsure how to reply. "I didn't feel I had much of a choice," he eventually said. "I didn't really have the opportunity to do much else. If I had your opportunity, I'd have grasped it with both hands."

"At least you earn an honest living."

"It's an honest job, but it's not much of a living. There's no future with this kind of back-breaking work. It eventually takes its toll and you don't have much to show for it in the end."

*　　*　　*

The company required workers at their other warehouse in South Melbourne. As the permanent workers were protected by the union, they had an option whether to relocate. The casual workers, on the other hand, did not have a choice. Two of the workers selected for relocation were Glen, as a forklift driver, and Art, as a labourer.

Glen and Art had a few things in common. They were of similar age – Glen was 25 and Art was 24 – they both lived in the western suburbs and they both had been foster children.

It was 1960 when Glen's mother had become pregnant at the age of 16 and was placed in a home for unwed mothers. Soon after his birth, Glen was placed in foster care.

Art was only a year old when his mother passed away, in 1962. The sudden death of his mother had a profound effect on his father as he fell into depression and became an alcoholic. Art was looked after by his grandparents until they could no longer manage and, at the age of three, he was placed in foster care.

Glen and Art took turns to drive to the company's warehouse in South Melbourne, where they took different routes in the effort to avoid heavy traffic. They often drove down Gertrude Street – the Black Mile – in the inner-Melbourne suburb of Fitzroy, where they observed Aboriginal people, many of whom appeared homeless.

"You have to feel sorry for the Aboriginal people," Art said.

"Why?" Glen replied. "They can get the benefits that other Australians can get."

"But they're not just like other Australians. They were the original owners of this land, which was taken from them, and they got nothing for it."

"Well that's life. The strongest survive and the weak are left behind."

"That's true for the law of the jungle but it shouldn't be the case in a civilised society."

Glen shrugged his shoulders.

"Do you know any Aboriginals?" Art asked.

"No," Glen responded. "Why, do you?"

"No, I don't. In fact, I don't think I've even spoken to one."

"Neither have I. Seems odd, never to have spoken to an Australian Aboriginal."

There was a period of silence before Art spoke. "We should take a trip to outback Australia."

There was another period of silence before Glen replied. "Yeah, why don't we?"

Chapter 3

An Outback Adventure

Glen and Art gained approval to take leave and they spent an inordinate amount of time organising their trip. They completed their packing by securing four jerry cans – two for water and two for petrol. At 10.00 am on Monday 7 July 1986, they took off in Art's panel van.

They alternated the driving, with Art taking the first stint. There wasn't too much traffic going their way as they travelled out of the city of Melbourne along Ballarat Road. They both had a big grin as they observed the heavy traffic going in the opposite direction.

As they continued driving along the Western Highway, the passing cars diminished, the spaces opened up and their smiles grew broader.

It was midday when they arrived in the former gold rush town of Ballarat.

"Have you ever been here before?" Art asked Glen.

"No," Glen replied. "Why, have you?"

"Yeah, I came here when I was a kid on a school excursion but we didn't visit the city. Instead, we went to Sovereign Hill where we did some panning for gold and experienced a re-creation of the gold rush days. It was good."

"How about we re-create the gold rush days by having some grub and a few beers at a pub?" Glen suggested.

Art grinned. "That sounds even better."

After a filling meal, they continued on their way, passing through the towns of Ararat, Stawell, Horsham, Dimboola, Nhill and Kiniva. It was past 6.00 pm when they drove over the Victoria–South Australia border and soon arrived at Bordertown.

"Want to stop for a feed?" asked Glen.

"I'd prefer to wait until we reach Adelaide," Art replied. "Although, we could celebrate our arrival in South Australia with a beer."

After their celebratory drink, they continued, weaving their way through the Adelaide Hills and on to Adelaide. They enjoyed dinner at a pub and found a hotel to spend the night.

The following day, they headed north, through Bumbunga, Snowtown, Redhill and Crystal Brook.

Glen was driving when he noticed that the temperature gauge had edged into the red zone.

"Looks like your car is overheating," Glen alerted.

"That's odd," Art commented. "The car's been running fine and the weather isn't hot. I just don't get it."

"Well, the gauge is well and truly in the red zone," Glen confirmed.

"You'd better pull over," Art instructed.

Glen stopped at a clearing and they both got out.

Art lifted the bonnet and he couldn't see anything abnormal. "There don't seem to be any leaks and the hoses look fine."

Glen placed his hand on the radiator cap. "Ouch! That's bloody hot."

"Clever stunt Houdini," Art joked.

Glen grabbed a rag from the panel van and returned to the front of the vehicle.

"What in the hell are you doing?" asked Art.

"I'm going to release the cap," Glen said.

"No way. It'll be too hot."

"Well I'm not going to wait all day for it to cool down."

"I'm warning you! Don't you dare release that cap!"

Glen ignored Art's comments and unscrewed the cap. As Glen sensed the pressure releasing, he jumped back. The cap popped off like a cork and dirty water spewed out of the radiator like a fountain.

They stood back motionless as they witnessed the spectacle for a few moments before the flow stopped. They then turned to each other.

"I told you not to take the cap off," Art said.

"Yep," Glen asserted, oblivious to Art's comment. "It must have been bloody hot."

Art took a jerry can of water from the back of the panel van.

"Start the engine," Art directed.

Art poured water into the radiator until it was full. He then took over the driving and proceeded very slowly. The temperature gauge was soon in the red zone again.

They puttered along, both not holding much hope of making it to the next town. When they finally limped into Port Pirie they stopped at the first garage.

"I can't help you, fellas," the mechanic said. "Your best bet is to try to make it to Port Augusta."

"That's around 100 kilometres away," Glen pointed out.

"Yeah, that'd be right," the mechanic replied. "You should take it easy and maybe open the heater vents to release some of the heat."

They slowly edged their way out of town,

proceeding steadily and slowly. They made minor progress with a one-hour drive taking aeons. They talked most of the way, repeating the same comments.

"The gauge is well and truly in the red zone."

"We've been travelling for ages."

"We're never going to make it."

After over two hours of driving, they finally made it into Port Augusta, again stopping at the first garage.

"I think your radiator's stuffed," the mechanic professionally advised. "I can order you a new one, which will take days, or I could fit a recore radiator tomorrow."

"I think I'll go for the recore," Art immediately decided.

Art and Glen spent the night at a motel and, after lunch on the following day, they returned to the garage.

"The car's ready to go," the mechanic declared as he wiped his greasy hands with a dirty rag.

Greatly relieved, they took off, leaving Port Augusta, the gateway to the north.

Glen took his turn at the wheel and his eyeballs continually glanced at the temperature gauge.

"How's it looking?" Art enquired.

"Looking good, Artie. Looking good."

They travelled through the town of Mount Gunson, stopping at Pimba for lunch. They continued on through Glendambo and arrived at Coober Pedy mid-evening.

They found accommodation hard to come by, eventually ending up at a caravan park.

"We only have a small on-site caravan available," the manager advised. "We keep it for storage, but you can have it for ten bucks a day."

Glen and Art inspected the caravan, which had a single bed and a lot of junk.

"If you're prepared to take the bed, I'll sleep in the panel van," Art suggested.

They accepted the offer and the caravan park became their home for the next few days.

The small desert town was unique, with most of the inhabitants living underground to escape one of the hottest and most inhospitable climates in Australia. It didn't come as a surprise to learn that in the local Indigenous language Coober Pedy meant 'white man in a hole'.

Taking a tour of the opal fields, Art and Glen were warned to be careful not to fall down a hole and were amused by a sign in the nearby desert, which read: *Keep Off Grass*.

They visited dugout buildings, including houses, a bookstore, a museum, an art gallery and a church, although they spent most of their time in a dugout pub.

Their last day in Coober Pedy was typically hot and dry, with a strong breeze kicking up the red dirt. They finished lunch and Glen went to the toilet while Art strolled outside and leaned against his panel van.

Art pulled out a cigarette, lit it and dragged in a deep breath. He exhaled a continuous stream of smoke as he looked around the eerie town.

A middle-aged Aboriginal man approached Art and leaned against the panel van beside him. The man had grey hair, a grey beard and many deep wrinkles lining his face.

"Gotta spare smoke?" the man asked.

"Sure thing," Art replied and tapped the top of his cigarette pack with his hand to fan out a couple of cigarettes.

The man selected one with his thumb and forefinger and placed it between his lips. He edged closer to Art, who lit the cigarette as the man inhaled. Art inhaled on his smoke and they both exhaled in unison.

"So, have you got a couple of bucks to spare?" the man asked.

Art turned to him and squinted, not knowing what to say.

The man smiled. "I was only joking," he admitted and started to laugh.

Art joined in, laughing.

The man slapped Art on the shoulder and trudged down the street. Glen arrived soon after.

"Ready to roll?" asked Glen.

Art smiled. "Yeah, I'm ready."

Chapter 4

Central Australia

The Stuart Highway led Art and Glen interminably north, when the sealed road suddenly turned to red dirt.

"I guess this is where the 300 kilometres of unsealed road starts," Glen said.

As they continued, the corrugated, loose and wet surface caused the panel van to vibrate and slide all over the road.

"We have to endure 300 kilometres of this battering?" Art commented. "I'm not looking forward to this."

They'd been driving for an hour when they felt a violent jolt.

Art slowed down, pulled over to the side of the road and got out to inspect the vehicle.

"We've got a flat back tyre," Art yelled.

"Oh yeah?" Glen shouted back from inside the vehicle.

"Aren't you going to get out and help?"

"I'm sure you can handle it yourself."

Art changed the wheel and they got on their way, Glen taking over the driving.

The road conditions got worse, with the road broken up in parts and holding large pools of water that looked like ponds.

Traversing through a body of water the vehicle stalled. Glen tried to turn over the engine. It started but, as he lifted his foot off the accelerator and onto the clutch to engage first gear, it stalled again.

They stepped out of the panel van into a foot of water and observed that the exhaust pipe was submerged.

Art took over the wheel and turned over the engine. It started and he kept his right foot on the accelerator pedal while he placed his left foot on the clutch to engage first gear. The vehicle slowly emerged from the water.

They were travelling at a good clip when they hit another pool of water and the panel van came to an abrupt stop.

"Bloody hell!" Art cursed. "What now?"

Art tried to start the engine, to no avail. It was dead. They got out of the car and Art lifted the bonnet. Neither of them was mechanically minded, but that didn't deter them from intently inspecting the engine. As they conducted their examination, a car drove up and stopped.

"Do you have a problem?" the male driver asked as a woman in the passenger seat peered over.

"Yes we do," Art replied.

"And we have no idea what it could be," Glen added.

"I know there's a garage a little way up the road," the man advised. "I can let them know that you need help."

"That'd be great," Art responded.

Almost an hour later a tow truck arrived, with the driver wearing a beaming smile.

After a quick inspection, the mechanic assessed that repairs would be required back at his garage. He then hitched the front of the panel van to the tow truck.

Glen jumped into the passenger seat of the tow truck and Art hopped into the driver's seat of the panel van before they headed to the garage.

"Looks like you've got a cracked distributor cap," the mechanic detailed after further inspection. "I've got the spare parts so I can have you on your way in a jiffy."

The mechanic carried out the repairs as well as supplying a spare tyre and they were on their way.

"We've only travelled less than a quarter of the distance of this trip and we've already had to replace the radiator, fix the distributor and had a tyre blow out," Art said in a downtrodden tone. "I wonder if we're ever going to make it."

They'd been driving a while, struggling in the dry, hot desert climate. The temperature in the vehicle was very hot, even more than they would have expected.

"I can't understand why it's so hot," Glen said.

"Yeah, I know," Art replied. "I'm sweating my arse off."

Glen looked over to the heater.

"You haven't got the heater on, have you?" Glen asked, half jokingly.

Art looked at the heater and observed that the heater vents were open.

"Bugger!" Art cursed. "We forgot to close the heater vents after the radiator was fixed."

"Fancy that," Glen said. "We've been driving through the desert with the heater on!"

*　　*　　*

It was mid-afternoon when they reached a non-descript place with a petrol station and a small pub. They filled up the tank and were heading towards the pub for a drink when they heard an Aboriginal man being turned away.

"Is the pub closed?" Glen asked the publican.

"No, the pub's open," the publican replied.

"So why did you turn away the other man?" Art queried.

"The Abos usually cause havoc when they've had a few drinks so we don't allow them in the pub," the publican explained.

"I guess it's better for them not to drink," Glen said.

"Oh no, just because we don't let them into the pub doesn't mean we don't sell them alcohol. We sell them booze out the back."

Art and Glen walked to the back of the pub, where they saw a few Aboriginal men in ripped old jeans and T-shirts queued up at a hatched hole in the wall.

Art and Glen walked to the front of the pub and continued on to the panel van.

"Aren't you coming in for a beer?" the publican called out.

"No," Art replied, "not here."

They drove on and the red dirt changed back to bitumen, which drew smiles and sighs of relief.

They crossed the South Australia–Northern Territory border and stopped for an overnight stay in the town of Ghan.

The next day they came to the crossroad where they turned left from the Stuart

Highway and onto the Earnest Giles Road.

The road was unsealed so it was back to red dirt. The road had tinges of grey ash and was extremely slippery. Art was driving all over the road. It took them ages to travel the meagre 12 kilometres to reach the Henbury Meteorites Conservation Reserve.

They took their time to stroll along the self-guided walking tracks, where they were intrigued by the craters, the largest 180 metres wide and 5 metres deep.

"I don't think we should continue to Kings Canyon," Art suggested. "It's another 200 kilometres and I think this road is too treacherous."

"You're the one who had his heart set on Kings Canyon," Glen said. "I'm not fussed."

Art felt gutted with the thought of missing out on one of the highlights of the trip. Nevertheless, he drove out of the car park and turned back the way they came.

Making it back to the Stuart Highway, they drove onto smooth bitumen, drawing broad smiles again.

In under an hour's drive, they made it into

the beautiful town of Alice Springs. They booked into a motel and took in the sights around the town, including the Anzac Hill Memorial, dedicated to those who served in World War I.

After a couple of nights in Alice Springs, they pressed on north, with Glen taking the wheel, driving through Ti Tree, Barrow Creek, Tennant Creek, Three Ways and Elliot. They were passing through Larrimah when they noticed a sign reading: *Green Park Crocodile Arena FREE ADMISSION*.

Art looked over to Glen who returned the look with a grin.

They took a quick tour of the complex. Glen then urged for them to move on and he took the wheel while Art enjoyed a snooze in the back.

After driving only a short distance, there was an almighty thump. Glen continued driving as Art jumped from his slumber.

"What the hell was that?" Art exclaimed.

"We hit a roo," Glen replied.

"We hit a roo? Stop the car!"

Art got out and inspected the panel van as

he directed questions at Glen.

"What do you mean we hit a roo? How did we hit it?"

"A kangaroo was standing on the side of the road and, as we drove by, it seemed to take fright and jumped into the side. Then it just hopped away."

Art inspected the side of the panel van and noticed a dent and red splattering.

"The kangaroo must have been injured by the collision. I don't know why you didn't slow down when you approached it."

Glen just shrugged his shoulders.

Art looked around the area, but there was no sign of the kangaroo.

"Give me the keys," Art demanded and he took over the driving while Glen retreated to the back of the panel van.

Arriving at Mataranka, Art prepared to go for a swim in the thermal pools while Glen remained lying in the back of the panel van.

"Aren't you coming for a dip?" Art asked.

"I don't feel like it," Glen responded.

"It's one of the most popular attractions in the Territory. You should make the most it."

"I don't feel like it."

"Well I'm going in," Art said, "and I hope you change your mind and join me."

Art walked to the thermal pools and submerged himself in the warm, turquoise waters. He enjoyed a soothing and calming time swimming and floating around before he returned to the panel van.

"The thermal pools are great," Art told Glen. "You should check it out."

Glen was still lying in the back of the panel van. He turned his body away from Art and remained silent.

"They're also supposed to be therapeutic," Art added, trying one last time to tempt Glen into taking up the opportunity.

Glen was motionless and didn't say a word.

Art settled into the driver's seat and drove on.

Chapter 5

Northern Australia

Driving straight through to Darwin, they made a beeline for Lameroo Lodge, cheap lodging in the centre of town that was recommended to them.

The twin share was a rectangular-shaped room and painted light green, reminiscent of a hospital. Two single beds lined opposite walls next to two matching wooden cupboards with mirror doors. A large central ceiling fan dominated the room.

After settling in, Art went for a shower while Glen flopped on his bed, still upset.

Art was enjoying a warm shower when he

heard the voice of a woman calling out.

"Have you got any shampoo?"

Art stopped washing himself and wondered who the woman was talking to. Then there was loud banging against his shower door.

"Hey you, have you got any shampoo?" the woman demanded.

"You do know that these are the men's showers?" Art queried.

"Of course I do," the woman replied. "So do you have any shampoo or not?"

"Yes, I've got shampoo," Art responded as he placed the bottle under the shower door.

"What room are you in?" the woman asked.

"Room 215," Art hesitantly replied.

"Righto, I'll return the shampoo when I'm finished."

When Art returned to the room it wasn't too long before they had a visitor – a chubby, young woman with mousy brown hair and light blue eyes. She walked into and around the room as if she owned the place.

"So whose shampoo is this?" she asked.

"It's mine," Art replied.

The woman threw the shampoo bottle onto Art's bed.

"Who's he and what's his problem?" she asked as she looked at Glen lying on his bed.

"That's my mate, Glen. I don't know what his problem is."

"I'm not feeling well," Glen said.

The woman walked to the side of Glen's bed and looked him over.

"So what's wrong with you, then?" she asked.

Annoyed, Glen lifted himself onto his elbows and repeated in a firmer tone. "I'm not feeling well."

"Not feeling well." The woman leaned over Glen and gave him an almighty bash with her fist into his ribs.

"What do you mean by not feeling well?"

Both Glen and Art were shocked by the assault.

"That bloody hurt!" Glen exclaimed.

"Did that hurt, did it?" the woman said as she gave Glen another bash to the ribs.

"Bloody hell!" Glen yelled. "Stop punching me!"

Art cracked a smile.

"Stop punching you, eh," the woman said as she gave Glen another bash to the ribs.

Art then burst into laughter.

"Stop punching you, eh," the woman repeated as she kept on bashing Glen.

Glen continued pleading for her to stop as his voice echoed with every pounding.

Art carried on laughing and then Glen burst into laughter as he continued pleading for her to stop.

The woman eventually stopped.

"My name's Sheila and I'm in room 224," she stated and left the room.

"Looks as though you've found yourself a girlfriend," Art quipped.

*　　*　　*

Glen and Art spent the next day exploring the Darwin city and waterfront. Sitting at a pub enjoying a beer in the late afternoon, they observed a large truck with an open-caged trailer filled with Aboriginal men.

"What in the hell is that?" Art asked.

"I reckon they're workers being carted back

home after a day's work," Glen suggested.

"It looks like a scene from a third-world country," Art commented.

That evening, Glen and Art attended an Aboriginal dinner on the beach, where Aboriginal men wearing ceremonial dress of white body paint, red loincloths and red headbands performed a corroboree. They then feasted on dinner that was cooked in traditional earth ovens using heated rocks.

Returning to Lameroo Lodge late in the evening, Art and Glen received a visit by Sheila, who made herself comfortable in their room. They indulged in a few nightcaps, with Sheila and Glen soon hitting it off.

The next day, Art visited a number of travel agents to ascertain what tours were available. Glen had arranged to spend most of his time with Sheila, so Art booked tours to Katherine Gorge, Kakadu National Park, and Melville and Bathurst Islands on consecutive days for himself.

First up was the Katherine Gorge tour. At the end of the day, Art returned to the room to be greeted by Sheila and Glen, and gave them an account of his day.

"We departed Darwin in the morning and visited the Adelaide River War Memorial to pay respects to those killed during the 1940s Darwin air raids. It was really sobering to learn about those who lost their lives. Then we went to Nitmiluk National Park – it was beautiful. We spent the rest of the morning at Edith Falls, where we had a swim. It was cool in the water and we sunbathed on the rocks. We were all completely relaxed before the tour guide spotted some freshwater crocs, which got us all up and at 'em."

The excitement was evident in Art's voice as he enthusiastically looked over to Sheila and Glen but they seemed to be more interested in each other.

"After lunch, we took a Katherine Gorge cruise. We saw exotic birds, wildlife and more crocodiles. It really was a special day," Art said as he finalised his account, although his words seemed to fall on deaf ears.

The next day was the Kakadu tour. Art was picked up in a small van, where he joined an American family – Mum, Dad, two teenage girls and a younger boy.

They headed towards Arnhem Land, admiring the rugged scenery along the way.

"We're approaching Nourlangie," the driver advised. "This is where you'll be able to witness the rock art."

"Rock and roll," the boy instinctively called out.

"It's not rock and roll," the younger of the two sisters chided.

"Yeah," the older sister added. "It's rock art as in cave paintings."

As they left the van, the driver introduced them to their Aboriginal guide, who was dressed in a ranger's uniform.

The guide set off at a brisk pace with the group members lethargically following.

"The rock paintings have been estimated to be up to 20,000 years old," the guide said.

The group members looked to each other and their eyes opened wide. They then quickened to catch up with the guide to hear his every word.

"The art expresses Aboriginal culture and their connection to country. It also expresses the relationship of the Aboriginal people with the land and their spiritual heritage."

The guide provided a wealth of information as he pointed to the various X-ray paintings, stick-figure paintings and other paintings of food, animals and humans.

The group found the artforms fascinating and were enthralled by the spectacular landscape.

Ubirr was especially stunning. The guide continued his explanations of the paintings, which depicted stories of the law and creation.

Art was particularly intrigued with three of the paintings: an image of the nature and spirit force of the Rainbow Serpent, a painting of a thylacine, or Tasmanian Tiger, believed to have become extinct on the Australian mainland more than 2000 years ago, and an example of contact art depicting a white man, said to have been painted in the 1880s.

"The paintings provide insights into hunting and gathering practices, the social structure and the ritual ceremonies of successive Aboriginal societies," the guide explained. "They provide a window into ancient human civilisation."

The group was silent for a moment, seemingly trying to come to terms with the significance of what the guide had described. They then individually approached the guide to express their gratitude and each shook his hand.

The driver appeared and drove the group to their lunch venue before taking them to the launch area for a cruise on the wetlands of Yellow Water.

They took in the breathtaking scenery of the expansive waters and Twin Falls Gorge.

As they returned, the guide pointed out much of the wildlife, including the jabiru, a stork-like bird. He also mentioned that they should be on the lookout for saltwater crocodiles.

"There's a crocodile over there!" the younger girl shouted.

The older girl took a number of photographs until they neared the object, which was, in fact, a log.

"Terrific," the older girl said. "I just took a whole roll of film of a log."

After the tour, Art returned to his room to find Glen and Sheila. Even though Art was excited about his experiences that day, he made no attempt to tell them. He simply greeted them, lay back on his bed and reflected.

The following day was Art's day trip to Melville and Bathurst Islands. He was picked up and driven to Darwin Airport, where a DC-3 passenger airline – a Cheeky Charley, formerly a D-47 Gooney Bird – awaited the passengers.

After 15 minutes in the air they were preparing for landing.

The small group was met by their local guide, who escorted them through a Tiwi Aboriginal community. They were shown the village-like lifestyle and learned a little about their culture.

They visited the museum and early mission precinct, taking some respite from the hot, humid weather in the quaint wooden Catholic Church.

They saw Pukumani poles – decoratively painted funeral or grave posts – and then had some free time.

Art went for a wander and came across a small gathering of Aboriginal men. He stopped and looked in their direction.

"G'day mate," one of them said.

Art approached the small group and noticed some sticks stuck in the ground in a circular formation.

"What's that?" Art enquired.

"It's our friend's burial site," a man responded.

"Oh," Art said. "What are those things in the middle?"

"They're our friend's belongings," another man replied.

Art took a closer look and could identify a small record player and a few vinyl records.

The Aboriginal men walked towards the town and Art followed. The men entered a small building, although one young man stayed outside.

"What do they do in there?" Art asked him.

"We run a business where we make arts and crafts that are used in the community. We also sell them as souvenirs."

"That's great. That'd keep you busy."

"We operate the business during the dry season. During the wet season we go bush."

"Is alcohol a problem here on the island?" Art tentatively asked.

"Nah, not really. It's banned to bring alcohol to the island."

Returning to Lameroo Lodge that afternoon, Art expected to find both Sheila and Glen but Sheila wasn't there.

"Hello Art," Glen said.

"Hi Glen. So where's Sheila?"

"She's returned to Perth. How was your trip?"

"Why ask?. It's not as if you really want to know."

"Of course I want to know. I'm actually very interested."

"You wouldn't believe the fantastic day I've had!"

Chapter 6

The Return Drive

Glen and Art departed Darwin in the early morning, with Glen taking the first driving stint. After 12 hours they reached Devils Marbles – a conservation reserve containing an abundance of weathered, granite boulders.

They were astounded by the huge red boulders, which appeared perfectly rounded, with a couple of them that seemed to have been smoothly cut in half.

They reached Alice Springs in the late afternoon of the following day and booked two nights at the motel where they had previously stayed.

The next day, they headed west to explore the MacDonnell Ranges.

The Larapinta Trail ran for more than 200 kilometres, but they planned to restrict their walks to the two most popular sites – Simpsons Gap and Standley Chasm.

Simpsons Gap was only 17 kilometres away and they reached it at around 9.00 am. They took their time to follow a few of the walking tracks.

Returning from their walk, they instinctively stopped under the shade of a tree and sat with their backs against its broad trunk. They took in the peaceful surroundings and admired the vivid, contrasting colours of the deep blue sky, green foliage, red rocky hills and pale sandy ground.

"This is a special place," Glen remarked.

"It sure is," Art replied. "In fact, I think it's magical."

They returned to the panel van and proceeded to Standley Chasm, a further 30 kilometres away. They arrived around midday with the sun high in the sky and the sunlight filling the chasm.

There were hordes of tourists, although they made little noise. The crowds seemed to be mesmerised as they followed each other through the chasm.

Art stopped halfway and looked up, following the deep brown and red colours of the towering walls until they separated to reveal a lacuna of deep blue sky.

When Art arrived back at the starting point, he sat on a rock in a shaded spot and waited until he was reunited with Glen.

"That was fantastic," Glen remarked. "Don't you think?"

"Yeah, it was. Although, it was also kind of strange."

"What do you mean?"

"I don't know," Art said and reflected on it a little more. "I felt weird, which I can only describe as spiritual."

The next day, they departed Alice Springs in the late morning and arrived at the Ayers Rock Resort in the late afternoon.

They settled into a double-bunk bed in a four-bed dormitory and quickly acquainted themselves with their two middle-aged roomies – Roy and Jake.

It didn't take long before Roy suggested they go to the pub and they immediately set off.

"I can hardly wait to see Ayers Rock," Art said as they headed for the pub.

"You can see it now if you want," Jake advised.

"I thought we were miles away," Glen remarked.

"Yeah, we are," Roy said.

"But you can make it out from over that ridge," Jake added, pointing towards a hill.

Glen and Art climbed the small hill as they stayed focused on the top of the ridge. As their line of sight rose above the ridge's edge, the giant monolith jutting out of the flat earth came into view and their eyes widened.

"It may not look all that impressive," Roy called out. "But you have to take into account that we're about 20 kilometres away."

"I think it's very impressive," said Glen.

"Yeah, very impressive," Art agreed. "Especially given it's 20 kilometres away."

*   *   *

There was movement in the early morning of the next day as the tourists prepared to view Ayers Rock at sunrise.

Glen woke up Art and they quickly joined the convoy as they drove towards the rock.

Vehicles of all types moved in a cavalcade until they reached the car park. People quickly disembarked their vehicles and jostled for the best viewing positions.

It seemed to take an eternity for the sun to rise as the viewers focused on the dark brown natural sandstone monument.

The sun then started to emit rays of light over the horizon and the transformation began.

The rock quickly changed colour to a rusty brown to a bright orange and finally to a burning red.

The audience oohed and ahhed as the colours changed.

Once the colour of the rock settled, most of the crowd instantly returned to their vehicles, although some of the spectators, including Art and Glen, remained to savour the experience.

They went back to the resort for breakfast before returning to Ayers Rock for the climb.

Art looked up at the starting point, which looked very steep.

"I don't know whether I want to do this," Art said.

"They say the first bit is the hardest," Glen pointed out. "And there's a chain for a short distance at the start to assist."

"It's not the degree of difficulty in climbing the rock that concerns me," Art explained. "It's whether it's the right thing to do."

Glen proceeded to climb the rock and Art sluggishly followed. They struggled over the initial part but then continued more comfortably. They made it to the top in quick time to observe a bronze plate – a survey marker from the Department of National Development.

The bronze plate featured the cardinal directions and the notable landmarks surrounding the area.

Art grimaced at the bronze marker and then looked out to the surrounding views of a vast, seemingly boundless arid land.

Glen and Art spent little time on the top before making their descent.

Once they reached the bottom, they followed the Uluru base walks, where they were fascinated by the rock forms, caves and reflecting ponds.

They returned to the resort in time to freshen up and join the race to the viewing areas to observe Ayers Rock at sunset.

"The sunset is just as impressive as the sunrise," Art said. "It's just in reverse."

Glen and Art celebrated their uplifting day with dinner and drinks at the pub.

The next day, they set off to explore the Olgas, a group of large, domed rock formations.

They observed the unique natural beauty of the area before they took some time to admire the highest point of Mount Olga.

They returned to the resort for their last night at Uluru and there was much commotion.

"What's going on?" Glen asked.

"The north–south road is washed out due to the unseasonal rain," Roy advised. "So no one is permitted to leave."

"You've got to be joking," Art said.

"No, not joking," Jake replied.

"How long is the road going to be closed?" Glen asked.

"Nobody seems to know," Roy said as he shrugged his shoulders.

"Although, some people think it could be weeks," Jake added.

Glen and Art looked to each other and grimaced.

They spent the next few days sleeping in, walking around the resort and drinking at the pub. They were becoming depressed as they reflected on the prospect of having to spend weeks at the resort.

During the evening of the third day, a policeman entered the pub. "The Stuart Highway should be open in the morning," he announced, which triggered a cause for celebration.

The party was in full swing when Art went outside for a cigarette. An Aboriginal boy in his early teens quietly approached him.

"Can you buy me some grog?" the boy

timidly asked.

"You're too young to drink," Art replied instinctively.

"Here's the money," the boy said as he outstretched his arm to reveal the funds.

"I'm sorry. You should be spending your money and your time more productively."

The boy looked out to the darkness of the night and then looked back to Art with a forlorn expression.

Art returned the boy's stare, looked out to the dark wilderness and then looked back to the boy as Art's eyes welled with tears.

"Sorry kid," Art said and the boy walked away.

Art dawdled to his room with his hands in his pockets, his head bowed down, and went to bed.

The next morning, Glen got up with a spring in his step, while Art languidly followed.

"Did you have too much to drink last night?" Glen asked.

"No. I just feel a bit flat."

They left after breakfast with Glen taking

the wheel. They made it to the Stuart Highway and, soon after, were greeted by unsealed road.

"Bloody hell," Glen cursed. "There must have been an enormous amount of rain and the trucks have really cut up the road."

"Look out!" Art yelled. "Here comes a road train. Wind up your window!"

The road train ploughed through a pool of water. Glen hardly had the time to move as mud splashed through the panel van. Art and Glen looked at each other, both covered with mud.

Art took over the driving and slowly weaved the car through the pools of water and cut-up red mud.

Every time they saw a large truck or road train coming through, they drove to the side of the road and wound up their windows. When the mud settled, they wound down their windows and continued on.

Eventually making it back onto sealed road, with huge sighs relief they both got out and kissed the bitumen.

They spent a couple of nights in Adelaide

before making the last stretch of their trip back to Melbourne.

Art enthusiastically unpacked to admire his Aboriginal souvenirs and peruse the printed material he had purchased and collected over the course of his travels. He read the material with great interest, which did little more than whet his appetite.

Art was keen to learn more about the Australian Aboriginals, although he had great difficulty in finding literature on the topic, particularly about any time prior to British settlement. This surprised him, given that the Indigenous people of Australia were considered to be the oldest continuous culture on the planet. Nevertheless, Art roamed all the bookshops, libraries and universities in his area in an effort to obtain information about them. He was so absorbed and overwhelmed by the information he was reading that he started taking notes.

PART 2

THE NOTES

Chapter 7

Aboriginal History

The Indigenous people of Australia were believed to be among the earliest migration of people out of Africa, although the precise period of their arrival had been subject to much debate.

It seemed widely accepted that the earliest occupation in Australia was at least 40,000 years ago, although this was subject to the restriction of definite archaeological evidence, largely due to the limit to which radiocarbon dating could be reliably applied. However, a popular estimate for the earliest occupation appeared to be around 60,000 years ago.

At the time of British colonisation, the Aboriginal Australians maintained successful communities throughout the continent, from the cold and wet mountain ranges of Tasmania to the arid deserts of Australia's mainland interior and the hot and humid tropics of the north.

Aboriginal culture was not commonly considered to be a civilisation even though it contained the main elements. Art, songs, dances, storytelling, law and religion are all present in Aboriginal culture.

The British who arrived on the Australian continent in the 18th century described the land and waters as a wilderness uninhabited by humans.

The Indigenous people of Australia were described as hunter-gatherers who survived by developing an intimate knowledge of Australia's land, waters, flora, fauna and climate. However, they had a more sophisticated system that also included spirituality, society, languages, relationship to country and governance of law.

Aboriginal societies broadly operated on a

sexual division of labour where generally men hunted and women gathered. Surprisingly, it was the women's gathering that provided the bulk of the food supplies.

More than 200 distinct languages and many more dialects were spoken at the time of British colonisation. It was common for people to speak the language of their community as well as one or more neighbouring languages.

Australian Aboriginal literacy is also evidenced by the use of message sticks. These inscribed sticks were used for various purposes, including aids to memory, safe passage through hostile country and a means of locating waterholes.

There is also evidence that the Aboriginal people undertook various aspects of land management. They used fire to promote the growth of grass eaten by game animals such as kangaroos. They harvested and dispersed seeds to encourage the development of grasslands. They dammed and redirected streams, swamps and lake outlets for fishing.

The Aboriginal people on mainland

Australia ranged from semi-permanent communities to semi-nomadic and nomadic communities. Their way of life varied in order to adapt to the local environment and the available natural resources.

In the less arid seaside and river communities, where fishing provided a more regular food source, the Indigenous populations generally lived in semi-permanent communities.

Other Indigenous Australian communities were semi-nomadic, moving in a regular cycle over a defined territory in order to follow seasonal food sources.

In the more arid areas, Aboriginal people were nomadic, roaming over wide areas in search of scarce food resources.

The Aboriginal communities also used to interact with neighbouring communities in order to trade and exchange various artefacts, foods and cultural forms such as songs and dances.

Many Aboriginal people travelled long distances to trade goods, arrange marriages and participate in social and cultural activities such as corroborees.

Of utmost importance to an Aboriginal person is their place of birth, which determines their connection to the land and defines their place in the world. They regarded the land as their own since the Creation period – the time of the Dreaming.

Generally, an Aboriginal person was a member of a clan, which was identified by specific tracts of land – clan estates – that provided most of the resources they needed.

Where the required resources were not available within the clan's estate, they were gathered from elsewhere or bartered from neighbouring clan estates.

Moreover, the clan estates represented the land and people as a unified whole, which facilitated the fulfilment of both their material and spiritual needs.

Aboriginal clan societies operated on a number of different levels. In addition to the clan being identified with a particular area of land, all the individuals born into a given clan spoke the same language.

Different clans were connected in various

ways, such as language, marriage, social activities and religious beliefs. Clans were generally exogamous, so that when a man sought a wife he would not only look within their own clan, but also look to another clan, usually being from an opposite marriage class (moiety) or skin group.

Chapter 8

The Dreaming

The Dreaming is a complex network of knowledge, faith and practices that dominates all spiritual and physical aspects of Aboriginal life and emanates from stories of creation.

These stories tell how the ancestral spirits moved through the land creating the waters, landforms, animals and plants. The places where the ancestral spirits have been and where they came to rest is known to Aboriginal people, even to this day.

The Dreaming is used to describe the time when the earth, humans and animals were created. It is also used by individuals to refer to their own Dreaming or their community's Dreaming.

On a practical level, the Dreaming sets out the structures of society, the rules for social behaviour and the ceremonies performed in order to maintain the life of the land.

Aboriginal people often interpret dreams as being the memory of things that happened during the Creation period.

The linking of dreams to the Creation period has led people to use the term 'the Dreamtime'.

Each tribe has stories about the Dreamtime that are told to children, discussed around campfires, and performed through singing, dancing and acting during ceremonies.

The stories of the Dreamtime form the basis of Aboriginal religion, behaviour, law and societal order.

Images relating to the Dreamtime are a feature in Aboriginal artforms on weapons, utensils, body painting, ground designs, bark paintings and rock art.

Essentially, the Dreaming comes from the land. In Aboriginal society, people did not own the land. It was part of them and it was part of their duty to respect and look after the land.

The Dreaming is a powerful living force that Aboriginal people strive to maintain. It embraces the past, present and future as an enduring life force.

Chapter 9

Aboriginal Societies

At the time of colonisation, Aboriginal Australians comprised over 400 groups, each with their own language and traditions, in which case, they could have been described as a group of nations.

Aboriginal people on the southern island of Tasmania are estimated to have been separated from mainland Australia by rising sea levels 11,000 years ago and they developed their own distinct groups.

Aboriginal culture varies from region to region. Examples of this are provided by the two most iconic items of Aboriginal culture –

the boomerang and the didgeridoo. The boomerang was used in south-eastern Australia, while the didgeridoo was used in the extreme northern region of Australia.

The Indigenous people have complex laws based on the grouping of people within their society. They also have a complex system of kinship and community, in which everyone is related to everyone else.

An appreciation of the complexity of Aboriginal societies may be gleaned by an understanding of how their society is structured, which may be categorised in terms of physical, social and religious structures.

The physical structure is centred on a tribe, or nation, represented by a language group comprising people who share the same language, customs and general laws.

The tribe may number around 100 people and is made up of bands. A band usually comprised several families numbering 10 to 20 people. Members of the band joined together to hunt and gather food.

The social structure is based on the relationship between the people, which is sometimes referred to as a kinship system, that allows each person to be named in relation to each other.

The Aboriginal kinship system organises people's relationships, obligations and behaviours towards each other. This in turn defines matters such as who will look after the children if the parent dies, who someone can marry, who is responsible for another person's debts or misdeeds, and who will take care of the old and sick.

Comparing the Aboriginal kinship system with that of Europeans, an Aboriginal person will know who their birth relations are, being their birth mother, father, sisters and brothers. However, they may also consider extended family members as mothers, fathers, sisters and brothers.

When an outsider is accepted into a group, the person is named in relation to the members of the group, which allows the person to fit in.

The religious structure throughout Aboriginal Australia is divided into moieties, which divide all members of a tribe, usually into two groups. This is based on a connection with certain subjects such as animals, plants, places or other aspects of their environment.

Aboriginal religion is characterised by deities that created people and the environment during the Creation period – the Dreaming or Dreamtime – at the beginning of time.

Aboriginal people have numerous deities all over Australia, with each tribe having their own deities.

In many instances, these deities are regarded as direct ancestors of the living people. Hence, these deities may be referred to as Ancestral Figures, Ancestral Beings, Ancestral Heroes or Dreamtime Ancestors.

The images of these deities are often depicted in a tangible form, such as a form of a particular landscape feature or in a plant or animal form.

In Aboriginal religious belief, after a person's death, their spirit may return in human, animal or plant form.

Aboriginal people believe that many

animals and plants are interchangeable with human life through reincarnation of the spirit, which relates back to the Dreamtime when these animals and plants were once people.

The original form of subjects such as an animal, plant or other object is referred to as a Totem Being.

As well as belonging to one or other moiety, each person is also connected to one or more of these subjects, or totems. Each moiety will have specific Totem Beings belonging to it, which define a person's origins, their connections with the world and their relationships with the past, present and future.

Chapter 10

Aboriginal Art

The art of the Indigenous people of Australia has been described as a living art, an expression of life in the present commencing from the Creation period – the Dreamtime.

Aboriginal art belongs to the world's longest living art tradition, unbroken for thousands of years. It continues to survive and develop as it has passed down the generations.

The art of the Aboriginal people is an expression of the world's laws that emerged from the Dreamtime. These laws were placed there by their ancestors for the initiates, being those elders who had demonstrated their worthiness to know.

Aboriginal art is closely linked with the rituals, beliefs and philosophies of the people. Whether the subject is a living creature, an inanimate object or a heavenly body, there is usually a legend that explains the origin of the subject and the country to which it belongs.

The Aboriginal people practise art that permeates all aspects of their life. It is the critical medium through which they keep alive their philosophies, laws and stories of creation.

The main purpose of Aboriginal art is to tell stories through the use of symbols, which are used as a way of writing down folktales, the stories of the Dreamtime or the description of important historical events.

For the Indigenous people, art and life are interlinked. In traditional society, they used sacred objects in ancestral rites. They painted, etched and carved their weapons, tools and everyday domestic utensils.

Paintings decorated their bark huts, the surfaces of rocks and the ground. They carved reliefs on trees and scratched out ornamental designs in the sand.

In the past, and among traditional groups now, Aboriginal people painted their bodies for ceremonies. They colourfully and vividly painted finely sculpted mortuary totem poles. They painted their weapons, implements, sacred objects and dilly bags – traditional woven carry bags. They even painted the skulls of the dead.

Rock art is a form of a recorded document that Aboriginal people take as having the force of law.

Rock massifs containing shelters and overhangs are where Aboriginal people painted aspects of their country, beliefs, ceremonies, and hunting and food-gathering activities.

The paintings at these sites have been laid down over thousands of years. They include human figures wearing ceremonial costumes that are no longer worn and representations of animals that no longer exist.

Over time, art depicted changes as technology evolved. The spear thrower is absent in the older paintings, but is common in less old paintings. Simple hand-held spears illustrated in older art are replaced by more elaborate spears in less old art.

Arnhem Land in northern Australia contains the two large rock painting sites at Ubirr and Nourlangie.

According to Aboriginal belief, two ancestral beings, the Rainbow Serpent and the Cockatoo Lady, left their images at Ubirr as they passed through the area in the Dreamtime, or Creation period.

At Nourlangie Rock in Kakadu National Park, the Lightning Man is painted in a shelter.

Bark painting is one of the most characteristic of the various Aboriginal artforms. The colours used are yellow, red and brown from natural ochres, black crushed charcoal from camp fires, and white kaolin clay.

Bark painting is generally considered to be for education purposes, whether it be in terms of teaching others or to improve one's self.

Each feature and shape in a painting has a

precise meaning, which the initiates are able to decipher, while they remain a mystery to others.

Aboriginal art sometimes involves the painting of spirits depicted in human form.

X-ray paintings represent bone structures and internal organs of creatures, which is a technique often used for painting animals that provided Indigenous people with food.

Aboriginal people interpret all natural phenomena as manifestations of the spirits. For example, the Thunder Spirit is believed to cause storms and appears in paintings symbolising bolts of lightning and claps of thunder.

Among the most popular spirits are the spirits of the rocks – the Mimi. These are a race of peace-loving, shy ghosts who are seen only by children. They hide themselves from adults due to their shyness and physical frailty.

There are also some dangerous ghosts – the Maams or Mamandis. Deprived of repose in the "land of the dead", these ghosts haunt and disturb the living.

The practices of Aboriginal art have

survived to this day and have generally maintained the purity of their traditional forms, although they are now less frequently practised.

Chapter 11

Torres Strait Islanders

In earlier times, the Torres Strait Islands formed part of the one landmass linking Papua New Guinea to mainland Australia.

Notwithstanding certain similarities and connections with mainland Australian Aboriginal people, the Torres Strait Islanders have their own unique culture.

In the Torres Strait, each community was traditionally divided into a number of descent or clan groups.

Torres Strait Islanders believe in ancestral beings who crisscrossed the Torres Strait. It is through these ancestral beings that the Torres

Strait Islanders are thought to be linked to each other, as well as the peoples of southern New Guinea and northern Queensland.

These ancestral beings gave Torres Strait Islanders laws to live by and laws that taught respect for each other, the earth and the sea.

These ancestral beings were said to be shape-shifters – changing form from human to animal, reptile, bird or fish – which allowed them to exist on the earth, in the sea and in the air.

Torres Strait Islanders draw their spiritual beliefs from the stars of Tagai. They understand the world and their place in it through the tales of Tagai.

The Torres Strait Islanders are united by their connection to the Tagai, which consists of stories at the cornerstone of their spiritual beliefs. These stories focus on the stars and identify Torres Strait Islanders as sea people who share a common way of life. The instructions of the Tagai provide order in the world, ensuring that everything has a place.

*   *   *

In July 1871, the Reverend Samuel McFarland of the London Missionary Society, accompanied by South Sea Islander evangelists and teachers, set out to convert the Torres Strait Islanders to Christianity.

In defiance of tribal law, a warrior clan elder named Dabad welcomed the party as they landed on Darnley Island or Erub Island in the native language.

Even though the principles of Christianity were largely compatible with islander beliefs, the conversion to Christianity was considered to have led to significant changes that affected every aspect of their life from that time onwards.

On 1 July of each year, the Torres Strait Islanders celebrate the holiday with a festival for the Coming of the Light – the time when the light of Christ was brought to the Torres Strait. The festival includes a re-enactment of the arrival of the first missionaries.

Chapter 12

White Men Commeth

In 1768, the British government instructed James Cook to obtain "consent of the natives" prior to claiming any inhabited land. However, in 1770, Cook failed to follow the instructions to negotiate a treaty with the Indigenous people of Australia.

It is unknown what the population of Australia was at the time of British colonisation, although it has been estimated that in 1788 the number of Australian Aboriginal people may have been about 500,000. However, this number was reduced dramatically due to a combination of factors, including the spread of the white settlements, the reduction of hunting grounds, the spread of disease, land dispossession and violence against the Aboriginal people.

Indigenous Australians were traditionally semi-nomadic, while also being strongly connected to particular sites that comprised their tribal homeland. The land is fundamental to every aspect of their lives, whether economic, religious, artistic or legal.

The connections to the land are earthly, cultural and spiritual. They are complex connections that carry traditional obligations and responsibilities. These connections are fundamental to the identity of Aboriginal Australians, who are connected to the land through their Dreaming. However, much of the connection to the land was destroyed as British settlers spread through the continent.

Over the years, regional areas were cleared for agriculture, destroying food sources and sacred sites. British settlement proceeded on the basis of Aboriginal people's wholesale dispossession of their land.

Aboriginal people initially resisted the

takeover of their land. In many places they waged guerrilla warfare for lengthy periods; however, the resistance was futile against the spread of disease, the larger settler numbers and superior settler weaponry.

Complex familial systems broke down for many Aboriginal people due to a number of factors, including the removal of children, dislocation and institutionalisation.

Many Indigenous people maintained contact with their land by living on pastoral leases, government reserves or Christian missions.

Pastoralists were responsible for the distribution of government-issued rations to Aboriginal people who were too old to work. However, in practice, the pastoralists dispensed rations as they chose.

The economy of pastoral businesses took advantage of cheap Aboriginal labour, often withholding wages from Aboriginal workers.

Many Indigenous people lived in towns, the outskirts of towns, fringe camps, beaches and riverbanks. Those who lived in or on the outskirts of towns lost access to their traditional lands and their way of life. Ultimately, they also lost their identity and their self-esteem.

Before British settlement disrupted their way of life, the clans moved freely around their estates on a seasonal cycle.

Movement was a critical aspect of the Aboriginal way of life as they reaped the available resources in order to fulfil their earthly requirements and spiritual obligations, including engaging in ceremonial and ritual activity centred at significant sites.

As the white settlers occupied the land, it became increasingly difficult for the Aboriginal clans to continue to live as their ancestors had done for hundreds of generations over thousands of years.

Aboriginal people were denied access to land and resources they had long relied on, as the white settlers objected to the Aboriginal people moving through the land.

As white settlements and pastoralists grew and spread across the land with their sheep and cattle, more and more areas became closed to the traditional owners. Hunting and gathering activities were restricted as settlers and pastoralists denied Indigenous people the free use of the land.

The increasing herds of cattle and sheep grazing on the plains ate many of the plants that were essential sources of food and disrupted the way of life of the Aboriginal people, as well as the native animals.

Without access to important and sacred sites, ceremonies that were designed to ensure the continuance of the Aboriginal way of life could not be performed and vital resources could not be gathered.

The combined effect of these restrictions to customary practice was that the Aboriginal people were largely unable to fulfil their earthly requirements and spiritual obligations. This was exacerbated by the rapidly declining population. Men and women of importance were dying before their time and the knowledge was dying with them.

The British government attempted to civilise Aboriginal people by forcing them onto missions and protectorates in an effort to make them adopt the British way of life.

The missions and protectorates also served the purpose of separating the Aboriginals from the white settlers and the land. The primary purpose of the missions was to convert Aboriginal people to Christianity.

Attendance by Aboriginal people on the missions and protectorates was poor, as they attempted to cling to their traditional and customary way of life.

In Van Diemen's Land, Tasmanian Aboriginals were removed from their land and relocated to Flinders Island in Bass Strait. In the end, almost all the surviving groups of Tasmanian Aboriginals were sent to the island.

*   *   *

In 1886, legislation for Aboriginal people was passed in Victoria and Western Australia, the main feature of which was to remove "half-castes" from stations or reserves.

Under the Victorian Act, Indigenous people under 35 years of age who were of mixed race were legally white and could not continue to reside on Aboriginal stations.

The size of the Aboriginal population on the stations was subsequently dramatically reduced, which also resulted in a corresponding reduction in the labour force, with the remaining adult populations being too old for physical work. Those who were released from the stations were thrown into a white society, which had a devastating impact, particularly for those who were least able to support themselves.

The influx of the British and their occupation of the land had a profound effect, through the destruction of the Aboriginal way of life, their culture and individual identity.

The white settlements also introduced diseases to the communities. Aboriginal people had no natural immunity to these diseases so the death rates were high.

The spread of the white settlements made the Aboriginal people's plight to maintain their customary way of life impossible. The result was that their life was bereft of meaning, with many turning to alcohol. The loss of their traditional food sources made them resort to handouts.

The stark reality was that the development of the new nation-state was made on the back of dispossessing Aboriginal people of every aspect of their lives.

*　　*　　*

From the late 1800s through to the 1900s, governments controlled most aspects of Indigenous people's lives, which included their wages, pensions and endowments. They often received only a portion of what was due to them, with the remainder kept in various trust funds.

Much of that money was mismanaged or diverted to other government programs. They or their families were never shown what money was being held and what money was owed to them. This injustice has been referred to as the stolen wages.

In 1915, A. O. Neville was appointed as Chief Protector of Aborigines in Western Australia, where he presided over the controversial policy of removing Aboriginal children from their families. It was part of a plan to culturally assimilate Aboriginal people into the white community.

Neville had a three-point plan.

1. Full blood Aboriginal people would die out.
2. Half-caste Aboriginal people would be taken away from their mothers and families.
3. Marriages among half-castes would be controlled and intermarriage with the white people would be encouraged.

The ultimate objective of the plan was for the Aboriginal people to have never existed.

Between 1936 and 1940, Neville assumed the position of Commissioner for Native Affairs.

In 1937, Neville reportedly declared, "Are we going to have one million blacks in the Commonwealth or are we going to merge them into our white community and eventually forget that there were any Aborigines in Australia."

The government-appointed administrators exercised total control over Aboriginal people's lives. Families were separated, with the children incarcerated and forbidden to speak their native language.

Many of the languages and dialects were lost, with only a small number of them surviving to be fluently spoken. Increasingly, Aboriginal people tended to speak Aboriginal English.

There were many injustices perpetrated against Indigenous people, including curfews, seizure of property, censorship, food rationing, lack of privacy, financial control, imposed labour and arbitrary law-making.

*   *   *

In 1939, the Minister for the Interior at the time, John McEwen, announced a "New Deal", which reflected the Commonwealth Government's policy of assimilation.

The aim was to incorporate Indigenous people into mainstream Australian life through cultural and social assimilation. The corollary to this would be for the traditional Aboriginal social and cultural way of life to die out.

The policy required Aboriginal people to give up their culture, kin and history. They were essentially forced to become "white".

Where they achieved this transformation to the satisfaction of the authorities, they would be issued with an Exemption Certificate and allowed to live as a white person. Although they were formally relieved of the heavy restrictions placed on Indigenous Australians, in practice, they still faced the same segregation and discrimination.

During the same period, many children, particularly those of mixed descent, were taken from their families and raised by white people.

Chapter 13

Protectionism

In 1869, the colony of Victoria enacted the *Aboriginal Protection Act*, which was followed by the enactment of Protection Acts in every other Australian state, except Tasmania.

In Tasmania, most of the Aboriginal families had already been relocated and segregated from the non-Aboriginal population.

Throughout Australia, poor living conditions and diseases brought about by settlers impacted on death rates of the Aboriginal population. Malnutrition, crowded living conditions and diseases such as leprosy, smallpox and syphilis all contributed to the increased rates of morbidity and mortality.

The Protection Acts also established the Aboriginal Protection Boards. These boards aimed to protect Aboriginal people; however, under this system, Aboriginal communities were broken up, with many forced to live on missions and reserves.

These boards were state-run institutions that regulated the lives of Indigenous Australians. They were also responsible for administering the various Half-caste Acts where they existed.

Under the protectionist policies, the boards exerted extraordinary control over Indigenous Australian lives. This included control over their residency, employment, mobility, marriage, nutrition, social life, education, wages, sexual behaviour and cultural practices. It also included the responsibility for the removal of children – the Stolen Generations.

Aboriginal people were forbidden from practising their traditional cultural activities and languages. Thus, they were denied the right to speak their language, to have their tribal names and to participate in traditional ceremonies.

Protectionist policies resulted in Aboriginal people being confined to reserves and missions where their employment and movement were monitored. They could not leave employment without approval, travel without permission, drink alcohol or be legal guardians of their own children.

The policy of protection meant that Aboriginal people could be relocated to reserves and missions, which meant that they were forced away from their productive land.

Reserves were set up and funded by the government. They were run by managers who controlled Aboriginal people by administering their affairs. These managers implemented the protection legislation at the local level. The so-called protectors may have been local police officers or station owners in pastoral regions.

In some jurisdictions, such as in the Northern Territory and Western Australia, the Chief Protector had guardianship over all

Aboriginal children, assuming their parents' rights.

The Chief Protector had the power to move Aboriginal people into towns, place them on reserves and place them in jail indefinitely.

Legislation and policies led to forced removal of Aboriginal people from their ancestral lands. The placement of large numbers of different Aboriginal language and clan groups onto reserves or missions led to widespread familial, social and cultural disruption as well as conflict.

For the first time, people who would normally not have shared the same space due to kinship taboos and different geographical living locations were now forced to live together in the confined and controlled spaces of the mission or reserve settlements.

As Aboriginal people were not recognised as citizens, they were denied the ability to purchase land and were forced to remain on the mission or reserve, increasing their dependency and developing a welfare mentality for handouts, such as for food.

The policy of protectionism renounced the validity of Aboriginal culture and endeavoured to eradicate it from Australia, which had the effect to demean, demoralise and keep Aboriginal people impoverished.

The legacy of these policies has had an enduring impact on the self-esteem and identity of many Aboriginal people.

During the official British policy of protection, it has been estimated that by the year 1900 the Aboriginal population was reduced by 90 per cent, dwindling from around 500,000 to about 50,000 people.

Based on the trajectory of the population numbers from the time of colonisation to the early 1900s, it was commonly believed that the Indigenous population of Australia was going to become extinct.

Chapter 14

The Constitution

Before Australia became a federation, the country consisted of separate sovereign colonies. The Commonwealth was formed after each colony had passed legislation for the Constitution, which came into effect on 1 January 1901.

Prior to 1967, there were only two sections in the Australian Constitution where Aboriginal people of Australia were mentioned, section 51 and section 127.

Section 51 reflects the powers of the federal parliament to make laws for the Commonwealth – the "heads of power".

Aboriginal people were specifically mentioned under the "races" power in clause xxvi of section 51, which had the effect of excluding them from the federal power to make laws on their behalf. The clause included the following words:

> The people of any race, other than the aboriginal race in any State ...

Section 127 related to calculating the population of the states and territories for the purpose of allocating seats in the lower house of the federal parliament and for per capita Commonwealth grants. The provision stated:

> In reckoning the numbers of the people of the Commonwealth, or of a State or other part of the Commonwealth, aboriginal natives shall not be counted.

There were a number of notable historical events that occurred in Australia during the 1960s that were considered to have been influential in changing the attitude towards the Indigenous people.

In 1962, the *Commonwealth Electoral Act* was amended to give Aboriginal people the right to vote.

In 1965, Aboriginal people, non-Aboriginal

people and students staged a Freedom Ride through New South Wales to raise awareness about the levels of disadvantage and racism experienced by Aboriginal people and in support of Aboriginal rights.

In 1966, Aboriginal stockmen of the Gurindji people and their families walked off Wave Hill pastoral station in the Northern Territory to an important sacred site nearby at a place named Daguragu on Wattie Creek.

The strike was initially to protest against intolerable working conditions and inadequate wages, but developed into a seven-year struggle for traditional land rights.

It had been considered that the culmination of these events led to the Australian referendum that asked the question:

> Do you approve the proposed law for the alteration of the Constitution entitled 'An Act to alter the Constitution so as to omit certain words relating to the people of the Aboriginal race in any state so that the Aboriginals are to be counted in reckoning the population'?

In essence, the constitutional referendum was to include Indigenous people in the national census and to enable the

Commonwealth Government to make laws on behalf of Aboriginal people.

The referendum was overwhelmingly passed, with a 90 per cent yes vote. This resulted in the wording that discriminated against Aboriginal people to be removed from the Constitution.

As a consequence, there is no wording in the Australian Constitution that discriminates for or against the Indigenous people. In fact, there is now no recognition of Indigenous people in the Australian Constitution at all.

Chapter 15

Land Rights

The Indigenous people of Australia are an integral part of the land and the land is an integral part of them. If they do not maintain the land, they believe it will cease to sustain life. Without contact with their land or if they are removed from it, they cease to exist.

Aboriginal paintings may be interpreted as a form of title to the land. If the Indigenous people lose their title to the land, the paintings lose their meaning.

At the time of British settlement, there was some precedent in international law that supported the contention that the new sovereign was obliged to recognise the prior rights of the Indigenous people.

British imperial policy seemed to honour the prior rights of the Indigenous people through the treaties in various parts of the world, such as in North America and New Zealand. However, this obligation had been denied to the Indigenous people of Australia.

In fact, it was reported that James Cook was under instructions to negotiate a treaty if he encountered Indigenous people. However, Cook failed to follow these instructions.

It has been suggested that this was possibly due to the belief at the time that the continent was uninhabited. In other words, the land was perceived to be *terra nullius* and thus regarded to be an empty land except for flora and fauna.

Land determined to be *terra nullius* was considered to have no pre-existing human habitation and, on this basis, the British claimed ownership and sovereignty of the land. It may also have been upon this basis that Cook could justify his failure to negotiate a treaty with the Indigenous people.

* * *

On 6 June 1835, John Batman, an Australian grazier, businessman and explorer, struck an agreement with a group of Wurundjeri elders for the purchase of lands around the Yarra River in south-eastern Australia. The agreement came to be known as "Batman's Treaty".

The treaty was widely disputed, with suspicions that the signatures of the Wurundjeri elders were, in fact, made by one of the five Aboriginal men who accompanied Batman.

Furthermore, since Batman, the Aboriginal men who accompanied him and the Wurundjeri elders did not speak the same language, it was suspected that the Wurundjeri elders did not understand the treaty or its significance.

The New South Wales Governor at the time, Richard Bourke, issued a proclamation that was approved by the Colonial Office of the British government on 10 October 1835. The effect of the proclamation was to make void any treaty, bargain or contract with

Aboriginal people for the purchase of land. The proclamation therefore made Batman's Treaty void.

More significantly, the proclamation was to formally implement the concept of *terra nullius*, which reinforced the view that the land belonged to no one prior to Britain taking possession.

As British settlement overtook the harbours, the good farming land and the fertile grazing land, the Indigenous people were deprived of their way of life, became hangers-on and became involved in uneven clashes with the white settlers. As a result, the Indigenous people declined rapidly, with almost all of the people who remained being those of mixed blood.

In subsequent court cases, the Australian courts held, on the settlement of the colonies, that Britain acquired not only sovereignty but full ownership of the land, which it was then free to deal with in any manner it pleased.

By 1910, all usable Aboriginal land had been taken by colonists or the Crown.

*   *   *

Aboriginal people fought in every war in which Australia had been engaged and often with great distinction. Even though they were legally excluded from serving in the armed forces, Aboriginal men fought at Gallipoli and other theatres of World War I.

After World War I, the returning Australian soldiers and their families were given reserve land by the government in recognition for their service. However, Aboriginal men who fought in the same war were denied the rights given to other returned servicemen. They were not entitled to land and received nothing.

This government policy resulted in further dispossession of the Aboriginal people as they could not return to their traditional lands. It resulted in forced migration into towns and cities, where they were not welcomed.

Even so, in World War II, as many as 6000 Aboriginal and Torres Strait Islander people enlisted. They took part as servicemen, servicewomen, members of irregular forces or in support units.

*　　*　　*

Vast quantities of bauxite were discovered in the 1950s on Yolngu land on the Gove Peninsula in north-eastern Arnhem Land.

In 1963, without consulting the original owners of the land – the Yolngu people – the Commonwealth Government authorised prospecting by Pechiney, a French company.

Later that year, the Yolngu people presented a petition in response to the threat of bauxite mining on their country.

The petition comprised a traditional bark painting revealing the people's relationship to the land, with explanatory text typed on paper in the English and Gumatj languages. The traditional documents were the first of their kind to be recognised by the Commonwealth Parliament.

In 1966, the mining lease was transferred from Pechiney to a consortium of Swiss and Australian companies operating as Nabalco.

In 1968, the Yolngu people took the Commonwealth and Nabalco to court in the first land rights case in Australian history: *Milirrpum v Nabalco* (1971) – the Gove land rights case.

The case was unsuccessful, but was thought to have paved the way for subsequent action for the recognition of land rights in Australia.

On Australia Day, 26 January 1972, in response to the finding in the Gove land rights case, William McMahon, the then Prime Minister, stated that the Yolngu people did not hold rights to ownership of the lands and waters.

The McMahon government rejected land rights in favour of conditional 50-year leases to Aboriginal communities, without giving them any rights to mineral and forestry resources.

Also on 26 January 1972, a number of Indigenous Australian activists erected a beach umbrella and the sign "Embassy" to represent a displaced nation on the lawns of Parliament House at King George Terrace in Canberra.

The beach umbrella was soon replaced by several tents and numerous supporters came from all parts of Australia. It was the birth of the Tent Embassy.

In February 1972, the protesters at the

Tent Embassy issued a petition detailing a five-point plan.

1. Aboriginal ownership of existing reserves and settlements.
2. Legal title and mining rights to areas in and around all Australian capital cities.
3. Compensation for lands not returnable.
4. Preservation of all sacred sites.
5. Full rights of statehood for the Northern Territory.

The demands were rejected but, despite various attempts to dismantle the Tent Embassy using local ordinances and police force, it survived and emerged as a powerful symbolic site.

* * *

Subsequent to the passing of the 1967 referendum, which allowed the federal government the power to pass laws on behalf of Aboriginal people, the government established the Council for Aboriginal Affairs, which was comprised of three non-Aboriginal men, and also established the Office of

Aboriginal Affairs.

In 1972, the Whitlam government abolished the White Australia policy. At the same time, the government introduced a policy for Aboriginal self-determination. The change was to provide for the right to cultural and linguistic maintenance and management of natural resources on Aboriginal land.

In 1973, the Whitlam government established the Department of Aboriginal Affairs, which took over from the Council for Aboriginal Affairs and the functions of the Office of Aboriginal Affairs.

The Department of Aboriginal Affairs employed Aboriginal people and provided advice to the government on Aboriginal Affairs policy. As a result, for the first time Aboriginal people had some voice towards self-determination.

The Whitlam government's policy of self-determination required the Commonwealth to support decision-making by Indigenous communities themselves and to relinquish the control that previous governments had wielded over their lives.

Under the policy of self-determination, the government also established Aboriginal Legal Aid, Aboriginal medical services and housing schemes.

When the Whitlam government was elected, rather than introduce national land rights law, it chose to establish a precedent by introducing land rights legislation in the Northern Territory, which was controlled by the Commonwealth.

In February 1973, Justice Woodward was appointed as Aboriginal Land Rights Commissioner to inquire into appropriate ways to recognise Aboriginal land rights in the Northern Territory.

In July 1973, Justice Woodward handed down his first report, which recommended the establishment of a Northern Land Council and a Central Land Council in the Northern Territory.

Aboriginal land councils were designed to give Aboriginal people a voice on issues affecting their lands, seas and communities.

In April 1974, Woodward presented his second and final report.

Based on Woodward's recommendations, the Whitlam government introduced legislation. The Bill was before the parliament when the government was dismissed in the constitutional crisis of November 1975.

Despite election campaign promises that the Bill would be passed without amendment, the new Fraser government buckled to pressure from the mining and pastoral industry groups as well as conservative politicians in the Northern Territory.

The *Aboriginal Land Rights (Northern Territory) Act* (Cwlth) passed in December 1976 and came into force on 26 January 1977. The legislation established the basis upon which Aboriginal people in the Northern Territory could claim rights to land based on traditional occupation.

During the 1970s, in a move back to country, many Indigenous people left the Northern Territory towns and mission settlements and moved to outstations on ancestral lands.

On the outstations, the Aboriginal people could attempt to reconnect with the land and maintain their culture without the interference and conflicts of modern town life.

On 1 July 1978, the Northern Territory was granted self-government.

In 1983, the boundaries of local Aboriginal land councils were set in the *Aboriginal Land Rights Act*.

∗   ∗   ∗

In the 1950s, the Australian government decided to set aside Maralinga, part of the Woomera Prohibited Area, for British nuclear testing.

Maralinga was in a remote part of South Australia, the home of the Maralinga Tjarutja Aboriginal people.

Part of the government's decision was to forcibly remove the community at Ooldea and resettle them further south at Yalata. The move and subsequent government action would prove disastrous for the community.

Between 1956 and 1957, seven atomic bombs were exploded on Maralinga land. There were further minor trials over the period from 1957 to 1962, where plutonium was dispersed over much of the land.

A clean-up was attempted in 1967.

The nuclear tests were to be kept secret; however, in the 1970s, a whistleblower spoke out to the media.

It wasn't until the McClelland Royal Commission of 1984-85 that there was an investigation into the nuclear tests, with the report delivered in 1985.

In January 1985, the Maralinga Tjarutja native land title was handed back to the Maralinga people under the *Maralinga Tjarutja Land Rights Act* (South Australia).

At the time when the land was handed back, there was no compensation paid to the Aboriginal owners. It was largely suspected that the land was still contaminated.

*   *   *

In 1982, a case was launched in the High Court by Mer Islanders Reverend Dave Passi, Celuia Salee, James Rice and Edward Koiki Mabo.

In 1985, the Queensland government attempted to kill off the court action by passing a statute declaring that, in 1879 when the islands were annexed to Queensland on behalf of the Crown, any prior rights of the Meriam people were extinguished.

The High Court held that the Queensland Act was invalid as it was inconsistent with the *Racial Discrimination Act 1975* (Cwlth). This allowed the case launched by the Mer Islanders to fight for their land rights to continue.

*   *   *

In 1985, Uluru was offered to be officially transferred to the Aboriginal people on the condition that there was continued access to Ayres Rock.

The Deed of Grant to Uluru National Park was delivered to the Uluru-Kata Tjuta Aboriginal Land Trust under the *Aboriginal Land Rights (Northern Territory) Act 1976*. The traditional owners then leased the park back to the Australian National Parks and Wildlife Service for 99 years, with the park's board becoming majority Aboriginal. It was one of the first parks in the world to be managed by a board with a majority of traditional owners.

*   *   *

113

During the 1983 federal election, the Hawke government had promised legislation to ensure land rights to Aboriginal and Torres Strait Islander people throughout Australia.

In February 1985, the Hawke government announced a new, revamped Preferred National Land Rights Model, which dramatically reduced the land rights initially promised.

The Burke Western Australian government, backed by the mining and pastoral industries, campaigned against the proposed legislation. In addition, the mining industry ran a multi-million-dollar advertising campaign against land rights.

In the face of the public scare campaign, as well as pressure from the Western Australian government and the mining lobby, the Hawke government did a backflip on its own commitments, which effectively put a stop to national land rights.

PART 3

THE STORY ENDS

Chapter 16

Leaving Australia

Glen returned to work at the South Melbourne warehouse after four weeks away.

Art took an extra couple of weeks off, which he used to complete his reading into the Indigenous people of Australia. When he returned to work, he was sent back to Footscray, where he was reunited with Hamish.

"How was your trip?" Hamish asked.

"It was great," Art replied. "I've really grown a strong respect for the Aboriginal people and their culture. It's something I never had anticipated."

Other workers overheard Art's discussion with Hamish and were quick to react.

"You've got to be joking," one worker commented. "The only culture the Abos have is a culture of alcoholism."

"What about the unique Aboriginal culture of art, language and way of life they developed over thousands of years before the white man came?" Art responded. "The only problem with alcoholism I saw was when Aboriginal people came in contact with the white man."

"Abos are all bludgers!" another worker argued.

Art again retaliated. "Based on what I saw, the Aboriginal people are prepared to work. It seemed to me that it just depended on whether they were given the opportunity."

"You can't blame the Aboriginal problems on the white man," yet another worker contended.

"I'm not blaming anyone," Art affirmed. "I'm just describing what I saw."

Art tried to explain what he had experienced on his holiday but he was always met with disbelief or disagreement. He couldn't understand why most of the workers seemed to have preconceived negative ideas about Aboriginal people.

The workers continued with their critical sentiments, which were scathing and relentless.

"It's said that racism is mainly born out of ignorance," Hamish told Art. "So you might be wasting your time with this lot."

Art considered what Hamish said was true and he tried his best to ignore the ongoing taunts but he still found the continuing negative attitude and intimidating remarks by the workers to be most upsetting.

"Abo lover" and "black brother" were two of the names that Art was called on a regular basis. Although he resisted reacting, he nevertheless found the comments to be increasingly distressing.

*　　*　　*

On 29 November 1986, Pope John Paul II addressed the Aboriginal and Torres Strait Islander people at Blatherskite Park in Alice Springs.

Art obtained a transcript of the speech as

he was eager to ascertain what messages the Pope had for them.

Art was heartened from the introductory message of how much the Church esteemed and loved them, and how much the Church wished to assist in their spiritual and material needs.

Art read the ensuing paragraphs with growing optimism, especially when the Pope reconciled the Aboriginal Dreaming with God's Spirit and creation. However, Art's mood noticeably changed when he read the remainder of the address.

The speech went on to note another people who came to Aboriginal land nearly 200 years ago. That the Aboriginal people had been dispossessed of their traditional lands and separated from their tribal ways with discrimination caused by racism being a daily event. The speech acknowledged that they had learned how to survive, that they still had the power to be reborn and that the time for this rebirth was now!

Art was most troubled as he continued reading. The address communicated that the

Gospel of our Lord Jesus Christ spoke all languages and that the Gospel invited them to become Aboriginal Christians. "To develop in this way," the Pope said, "will make you more than ever truly Aboriginal."

Art didn't know how he was supposed to interpret the concluding statements; however, his overwhelming feeling was that it conveyed the messages to celebrate their survival, but to move on by adopting the white man's beliefs. He took this to be another form of dispossession.

*   *   *

Over a period of months, Art found the taunts by many of his co-workers to be cutting. He became depressed and had trouble sleeping. He only managed to get a couple of hours sleep on weeknights, which he attempted to make up for on weekends.

Art found that he was always sleeping in and struggled to get out of bed. It was a situation he persevered with through the remainder of 1986 and throughout 1987.

Towards the end of 1987, there was much hype as Australia was to celebrate its bicentennial.

The Aborigines declared their opposition with protests. "White Australia has a black history" and "Australia Day equals Invasion Day" were messages that some Aboriginal people declared.

On 26 January 1988, thousands of Aboriginal and Torres Strait Islander people and their non-Indigenous supporters marched through the streets of Sydney, as they did all over the country. However, they did not celebrate the day as Australia Day; they celebrated the day as Survival Day.

The workers at the Footscray warehouse directed their opposition to the march against Art. He would not be drawn into the arguments but he felt the pain of hate in their sentiments.

Art got to the point of physical and mental exhaustion and decided to take leave. He planned to take seven months off work and escape overseas.

Hamish was the only worker at the Footscray warehouse who Art confided in about his leave and, at the end of Art's last day at work, on Friday 11 March 1988, Hamish quietly wished him farewell.

The following Sunday, Art took a taxi to Melbourne international airport. He marched into the terminal saddled with his backpack, clasping his passport in one hand and an around-the-world airline ticket in the other.

Art knew the direction he was going to fly and had a rough idea of the countries he wished to visit. However, his main objective was to simply take a break out of Australia.

Chapter 17

Returning Home

Art arrived back in Australia on 12 August 1988, two months before he was due back at work. He thoroughly enjoyed his world-wide travels, which had taken his mind off his worries, but the moment he landed back in Australia his depression returned.

Art's sleeping pattern was unpredictable and he was feeling unwell so he decided to visit his doctor.

Art provided a description of his condition and waited patiently for the doctor's diagnosis and advice.

"What about your parents?" the doctor

asked.

"Both of my parents have passed away."

"Do you live with anyone?"

"No, I live alone."

"Do you have any family and, if so, do you see them much?"

"No. I don't have any other family members."

"What about friends?"

"I've got university mates and a couple of friends at work but I haven't seen them since I've been on leave."

The doctor took a long stare at Art before he gave his recommendation.

"You might want to reconnect with your university friends and your workmates before you go back to work. I'm sure they would appreciate seeing you and you could do with their company."

The doctor further deliberated before he continued.

"I'm reluctant to prescribe sleeping pills given that you live alone and that you feel depressed. However, I believe you would benefit from counselling so I'll provide you with the details of a couple of psychologists."

Art considered socialising with his friends from university but he didn't feel up to it. He also thought about meeting up with Hamish and Glen, but he felt uncomfortable reconnecting with them prior to returning to work and decided against it. He didn't bother with the psychologists.

Instead, Art began drinking, which was the only way he found he could get some sleep. Even so, he was experiencing long, restless nights.

Chapter 18

Our Republic

The alarm went off and Art jumped out of bed. He threw on his clothes, grabbed his coffee thermos and rushed off to work.

It was a cold and misty winter morning. Art joined the crowd of workers as they jockeyed for position outside the main gates of the Footscray warehouse.

Art sipped on his coffee, which gave off steam as it became exposed to the cold air. Catching a glimpse of Glen from the corner of his eye, he set off to greet him.

"Hey Glen!"

"Hi Art, how was your overseas holiday?"

"It was great," Art spontaneously replied. "So what's new?"

"Nothing much. Other than Australia becoming a republic, of course."

"Australia becoming a republic," Art repeated as he chuckled. "What in the hell are you talking about?"

"We now have an Australian Republic," Glen confirmed. "I'm amazed you haven't heard."

"I've been overseas, but I can't believe I didn't hear anything about it."

"Well, we have a republic with a president."

"What about all the problems that were raised about a new constitution, replacing the governor-general and how a president would be appointed."

"The penny seemed to drop when it was realised that Australia would never truly advance and reach its full potential until it accepted that the Aboriginal culture was Australia's original and true culture," Glen said. "It then seemed to be a natural progression for us to embrace the Aboriginal culture and to reconcile with the Aboriginal people."

"I don't understand," Art admitted. "How has Australia embraced the Aboriginal culture and what's this got to do with Australia becoming a republic?"

"Australia has elevated the importance of Aboriginal culture, including their history, language, music, dance, art and way of life, to the same level as the white man's culture," Glen advised. "This has resulted in government providing an equivalent level of support to programs covering all aspects of Aboriginal cultural endeavours in various areas, such as in education, training, business and social. Similarly, the private sector has grasped opportunities to promote Aboriginal culture nationally and internationally. The upshot of all of this has been job opportunities for Aboriginals with their unemployment numbers dwindling."

"This is unbelievable," Art mumbled. "What about the Australian president?"

"The president effectively took over a similar role to the governor-general as the ultimate figurehead of the nation, which turned out to be a very smooth transition," Glen explained. "However, rather than being appointed by the Queen on the advice of the prime minister, the president is appointed by the prime minister on the advice of Aboriginal elders."

"Are you saying that the president of Australia is Aboriginal?" Art quietly asked with eager anticipation.

Glen slowly nodded with a smile.

"This is fantastic!" Art exclaimed as he looked to the sky. When he looked back, Glen was on the move.

"Well, neither of us has been selected to work today," Glen called out, his voice diminishing as he walked away.

"Hang on Glen!" Art shouted out as he attempted to reach Glen through the moving crowd. "I want to know more about the republic!"

Glen continued walking away as if he couldn't hear him.

"Hang on!" Art yelled as he continued to fight through the crowd. "What about other issues concerning Aboriginal communities like the black deaths in custody, the forced sterilisation of Aboriginal women, the institutional racism in Aboriginal health, and land rights?"

With each point that Art raised, he felt an increasing crowd crush to the point where he was having trouble breathing, he couldn't free his arms and could no longer move.

Glen was out of sight and Art increased his intensity to extricate himself from the crowd, but to no avail.

"Wait! Wait!" Art repeated shouting as he continued fighting against the resistance with rising panic and frustration. He wriggled and struggled to break free, and then he snapped out of it with a violent jolt.

Art was sitting up on his bed, wrapped up in his bed sheets and drenched in sweat. He looked into the mirror on top of the dressing table set away from the foot of his bed. He witnessed his reflection with bloodshot eyes, five o'clock shadow and face dripping in perspiration.

Art then looked to his bedside table to observe an ashtray filled with butted out cigarettes and an empty bottle of scotch. As he came to his senses, he realised that Australia was not a republic. He had been dreaming.

Chapter 19

Our Country

Art was traumatised by his dream and he developed unhealthy lifestyle habits. He would sleep in until the late afternoon, when he would step out for some fast food and return to his unit armed with his daily supply of booze – a six-pack of beer and a bottle of scotch.

Art was alone and wouldn't visit anyone. The thought of socialising or coming into contact with people upset and angered him.

Art's best friend was his alcohol, which he would savour as he slowly drank throughout the day. One day rolled into the next.

Art was well aware he was in a rut, but he found it hard to get out of. If he was to be honest with himself, it was a self-inflicted rut that he didn't really want to get out of.

Being sober would accentuate Art's biggest fear: the full realisation of the dire plight of the Indigenous people of Australia, which he sensed would never be redressed.

Art polished off his daily ration of beer and scotch, and fell into a deep sleep. He woke up early in the morning and heard birds chirping. He peered outside his front bedroom window to see a clear, blue sky and admired the tree branches as the leaves wavered in the breeze.

Art forced himself to get out of bed. He washed up, dressed and walked out onto the front porch, where he raised his hands to shade the bright sunlight from his eyes.

Art looked across to the nearby park and, as if he was in a trance, he started trudging towards it. As he arrived at the park, he noticed some movement near the bank of the river.

Art slowly moved closer and camouflaged himself behind a tree. He then lowered a small, leafy branch to widen his view.

Art identified a male Aboriginal elder sitting down on a blanket with a young Aboriginal boy. Laid out on the blanket was an object that Art could not make out.

"Red ochre is often used in ceremonies to show the Aboriginal spiritual relation to the land," the elder explained. "The red represents the red earth and our relationship to it. The yellow centre circle depicts the sun, which we respect as the giver of life and protector. Finally, the black colour represents the Aboriginal people of Australia."

The young boy was marvelling over the object, which was the Aboriginal flag.

"The Australian earth is red and Australia is sometimes referred to as the sunburnt country, so it's good to include the sun. The black colour represents the Aboriginal people, but it also looks like the night sky," the boy said cheerfully. "If it did represent the night sky, they could include stars."

"It's an interesting thought," the elder said. "However, if white stars were placed in the black sky, people may take this to represent white people joining with black Aboriginal people. Do you think white people have earned the right to be represented on the Aboriginal flag?"

The boy looked up to the sky as he thought about the question and then looked towards Art.

"What do you think?" the boy asked Art. "Do you think that white people have earned the right to be represented on the Aboriginal flag?"

Art was shocked that the boy knew of his presence and he took a step back in surprise.

"Yes," the elder said. "What do you think?"

Art steadied himself before he turned his mind to the question and he took some time to reflect. He bowed his head slightly and put on a serious and sad expression.

Art then slowly shook his head. He continued to shake his head as he then whispered, "No."

"No," Art started repeating in crescendo as he shook his head quicker. He then shook his head violently and spoke louder to the point where he shouted at the top of his voice,

"Noooo!"

At this point, Art found himself raised up on his bed, looking at himself in the dressing table mirror – an unshaven, uncouth individual with dishevelled hair, and perspiration sprinkled on his forehead and trickling down his cheeks.

Art stayed motionless, like a statue, fixated on the figure in the mirror.

After a few minutes, Art started to laugh. His laughter got louder and louder, to the point where he sounded like an out-of-control madman. In an instant, as he came to his senses, he stopped laughing and his expression turned solemn. He had once again been dreaming.

Chapter 20

An Awakening

Art had not had a drink in several weeks and got ready for work. He had a shave and a shower before dressing into a three-piece suit and tie. He enjoyed a hearty breakfast, collected his briefcase and drove off in the second-hand Alfa Romeo Sprint he had purchased the week before.

It was 8.00 am when Art left the house, being hours after the workers at the Footscray warehouse would have been selected for work. He parked the car outside the front gates and was allowed inside. He made his way to the storage shed where he had previously worked.

Art entered the shed and immediately identified a familiar face. It was Hamish working at his customary cracking pace. Hamish looked up with a puzzled expression and approached him.

"You're a bit late for work, aren't you?" Hamish asked. "And what's with the get-up?"

"I'm not working here any more," Art replied.

Hamish was confused and looked askance at him.

"I've managed to get a job as a graduate lawyer doing social work with the Australian government," Art advised.

Hamish cracked a smile and it was the first time that Art had witnessed his cigarette-stained teeth.

"That's fantastic," Hamish said as he took hold of Art's hand and shook it. "How in the hell did you ever manage to get that?"

"I expect the glowing referee's report I got from Murray might have helped."

"So our foreman's got a heart after all," Hamish quipped.

“I’d like to thank you for all your help Hamish,” Art said with a quiver in his voice, slightly choked with emotion. “You not only helped me with my labouring job, but you also opened my mind to other opportunities.”

“I’m really happy for you, kid.”

“I’m going to say goodbye to Murray before I head off to say goodbye to Glen. Why don’t you come with me?”

Art and Hamish walked on side by side.

Epilogue

Art left his labouring job at the Footscray warehouse to pursue a rewarding career as a lawyer, specialising in social work, human rights and legal aid.

Art made a large number of friends over the course of his legal career, although he considered his most valued friends to be Hamish and Glen, with whom he kept in regular contact.

Art found the woman of his dreams, or maybe she found him. Although they weren't able to have a baby, they adopted two beautiful children – a brother and sister – who would have otherwise been placed in foster care. It was more than coincidental that the children were part-Aboriginal.

Over his lifetime, Art travelled the world, but the trip he considered to be his most rewarding and profound was the trip he took to outback Australia.

The memory of the trip would never be lost on him and, even though he had stopped dreaming, he never stopped hoping for ultimate justice for the Indigenous people of Australia.

www.ingramcontent.com/pod-product-compliance
Lightning Source LLC
Chambersburg PA
CBHW071001120726
47910CB00004B/1326